Amy Asks a Question . . .
Grandma, What's a Lesbian?

Amy Asks a Question . . .
Grandma—What's a Lesbian?

by Jeanne Arnold

Illustrations by Barbara Lindquist

Mother Courage Press
1667 Douglas Avenue
Racine, WI 53404

Library of Congress Cataloging-in-Publication Data

Arnold, Jeanne.
  Amy asks a question—Grandma, what's a lesbian? / by Jeanne
Arnold: Illustrations by Barbara Lindquist.
  p. cm.
  Summary: Grandma Bonnie, who has been in a lesbian relationship for more than twenty years, explains to Amy about gay pride and
being a lesbian.

ISBN 0-941300-28-5

  (1. Lesbians—Fiction. 2. Homosexuality—Fiction. 3. Grand-
mothers—Fiction.) I. Lindquist, Barbara, ill. II. Title.
PZ7.A73545Am 1996
(Fic)—dc20   96-32240
                                                            CIP
                                                             AC

Library of Congress Catalog Card Number 96-32240
ISBN 0-941300-28-5

Mother Courage Press
1667 Douglas Avenue
Racine, WI 53404

*This little book
is dedicated
to Jeanne and Barbara's
six children
and eleven grandchildren
with our
mutual love and respect.*

It was a Mother's Day
visit to Grandma
Bonnie's house with
Mom, Dad, my little
sister, my brother and
me, Amy.

I like to go to
Grandma Bonnie's house
because there are so
many books to read and
projects to do. Last time I
was there I read from one
of her adventure books,
the big picture book
about sharks. Once I
made a headband from
her craft box of leathers,
feathers, fur chunks and
beads that she keeps
under her pool table in
the basement.

I like to visit with her
too because she talks to
me like I'm an adult.

During this visit, Dad asked my little sister to tell what was at *his* parents' house that Grandma Bonnie didn't have at her house. (He was thinking about the new tropical fish aquarium that we would soon see when we visited them later.)

My sister thought very carefully and, knowing that she had discovered the correct answer, proudly announced, "A grandpa!"

"That's right!" said Grandma Jo, who gave a long and hardy laugh at my sister's answer, "There's definitely no grandpa here!"

And my mom said, "Ah huh."

*****

On most visits to their home, Grandma Bonnie and Grandma Jo sit in their chairs and talk with my mom when they're not paying attention to us.

The adults talk over the noise of my brother and sister playing on the piano or the electronic keyboards or on one of the many drums in my two grandmas' musical instrument collection.

That's when their dog, Luv, hides under the dining room table.

Usually my brother and sister chatter while they rearrange the toys and travel souvenirs set out in front of the hundreds of books stacked tightly on the shelves lining the walls. While all that is going on in the room, the adults keep talking.

They think that I'm reading in my favorite chair in the corner of the family room and that no one else is paying attention to them. But I have heard things. Sometimes people talk over your head, not thinking you understand . . . but I am really listening to the stories that my mom and grandmas share.

* * * * *

One day, Grandma Bonnie told Mom that tomorrow they were going to the city to march in their first gay pride parade. Grandma Jo grumbled that she was getting close to her retirement years. She said, "So what could it hurt if I risk my job and come out to the whole world."

I thought, "What does 'gay pride' mean, anyway?"

Pride? I feel proud of myself when I get my good reports at my school, when I learned to play the flute, and when I help my mom and dad watch out for my brother and sister.

Grandma Bonnie is an artist. Her paintings fill the walls of their home.

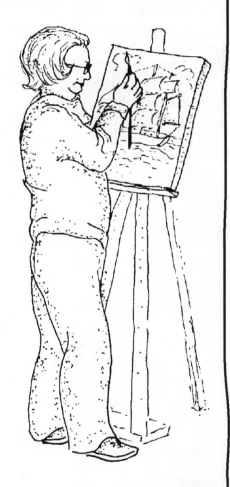

She is an author, a musician, a computer expert and a woman who owns her own business. And she's proud of all that. She's proud of all her four children and eight grandchildren. Why does she want to go to a gay pride parade to feel proud?

And Grandma Jo is proud, too. She's always showing us pictures that she takes of us and of her two children and her three grandchildren— and the pictures she takes of her friends and of her and Grandma Bonnie's trips to so many different places.

She's proud of her hospital work, too. We visit her in her office when we go to see our asthma doctor at her hospital. She wears business clothes there. When she's not at work, Grandma Jo wears Minnie Mouse and rainbow t-shirts and faded blue jeans, and she changes her hairstyle from a bun in the back into a long, single braid that hangs over her shoulder.

She's proud of her garden, too—even her compost pile.

Gay? I think I know what that means. My daddy's brother was gay. He and his friend were lots of fun when they'd come to visit us. My uncle had learned to sign for the deaf and would go to emergency rooms and to hospitals like Grandma Jo's to help deaf patients. He signed the words for

songs at places like concerts and festivals, too. I was proud of him. He died of AIDS. I miss him.

And what does *come out to the whole world* mean, and why would it *hurt* to *come out*, I wonder.

*****

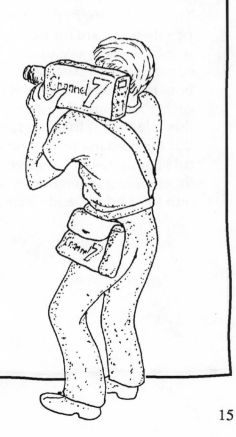

I've heard my two grandmas tell my mom stories about what happened years ago when Grandma Bonnie lost her job at their hospital, just after they bought their house and moved in together. Grandma Bonnie and Grandma Jo worked together there in the same department. They had thought that hospital people who care for people would be kind and understanding. They trusted their boss to understand why they each got divorced and why they wanted to live together. But the boss made up a new rule about co-workers living together just when they moved into their house, and Grandma

Bonnie got laid off—permanently.
They said it was a scary time.
They thought that Grandma Jo
would get fired too and that they
would run out of money.

But they were brave—so brave, in fact, they used some money they had saved and opened a women's bookstore. They did all the remodeling in the old building, even the carpenter work to build the bookcases. They installed a tall library ladder to reach to the top of the high shelves. They sanded and refinished the floors. It was a proud day when they put all their new orders of books on their shelves.

It was a prouder day
still when they opened the
doors for business.

Grandma Jo worked
hard to keep her job at the
hospital to help pay most
of the bills, and in her
spare time she used every
way she could think of to
promote the bookstore,
especially the free ways.

She said her boss didn't like it when she wrote letters to newspapers that printed her opinions on equal rights for women and on the church and women. She said she really got in trouble when she wrote a letter to try to stop a make-believe witch burning at the town's annual Halloween bonfire.

"We became too visible, again, I guess," said Grandma Jo.

*****

Recently I heard Grandma
Bonnie and Grandma Jo
talking about celebrating
their handfasting after 20
years of loving each other.
I guess it's kind of like a
wedding ceremony with
their woman friends at what
they call "their moon circle."
They described the
ceremony, what they said
to each other and how their
friend in charge of the ceremony was dressed in a
flowing lavender robe with
stars and moons sewn on it.
They said they did some-
thing called, "jumping over a
broom," and then they had a
big party.

I wish I had been there.
When they were talking about this, my mom
kept saying, "Ah huh."

*****

One Saturday morning, my mom and I were looking out the kitchen window watching my brother and sister play with their friends in the back yard. After a little while I asked my mom, "What is a lesbian?"

"Amy. Why do you want to know?"

"Well, yesterday during recess, our girls team won our soccer game and I hugged Kathy—all the girls hugged each other, and some kids teased us and called us 'Lesbians.' I've been wondering about that and about the nasty way they said that word, and I want to know what that means."

I watched Mom reach for the phone to call Grandma Bonnie. Mom said to her, "Amy and I would like to come over for a talk. Is that OK? She has a question she wants to ask you."

Mom and I arrived in half an hour and Grandma Bonnie and Grandma Jo were waiting for us two. They were curious, but they took the time to get us some refreshments and we made ourselves comfy in our favorite chairs.

When we were settled down, I said, "Mom said I should ask you, Grandma. . . . What is a lesbian?"

"Well," said Grandma Bonnie. "We've been waiting for a long time for that question to come from one of our grandchildren."

Then she took a deep breath and said, "Amy, *we* are lesbians, Jo and I, and we're called 'lesbians' because we love each other. Lesbians are women who prefer to be with women as friends or who choose women as their lovers and/or partners.

Lesbians love women rather than or more than they could love men as lovers or as husbands."

Grandma Jo interrupted
Grandma Bonnie and said to her,
"But each woman needs to think of
herself as a lesbian before anyone
else can pin that label on her. You
are a lesbian only if you consider
yourself one!"

Grandma Jo shifted in her
chair, looked at me again and said
softly, "Your Grandma Bonnie and
I have loved each other for many
years. No relationship with a man
could begin to hold the heartfelt
and positive value in my life that is
possible with Bonnie."

"We've had our ups and downs
over the years," Grandma Bonnie
continued. "Though we were
excited and happy about finding
ourselves in love, we were very
uncertain and even afraid of those
feelings for each other. And we
were worried about what our
families and friends would do. We
were especially fearful that we
would lose our children because
we thought that they would reject
us. Telling our children about our

love was deeply emotional. They
and your mother were all teen-
agers then and we didn't know
how they would react."

And my mom said, "It was
hard for us to understand, and we
were afraid of what was going to
happen to us, too. And we didn't
know how our friends would
react, either."

Grandma Jo said,
"Those grim times shared
together challenged us and
gave us courage. Now we
have so much to celebrate
together."

And Grandma Bonnie
added, "We've worked
through all those fears, and
for years our relationship
has been very much like a
happy marriage. We
would get legally married,
if we could. We care for
each other and each others'
families, and we support
each other completely.
We've been thinking about
having our minister
perform a commitment
ceremony for us at our
church. We were going to
wait for our twenty-fifth

anniversary, but now that you better understand our lives together, we may do that soon, and you and all our children and grand-children, other relatives and friends can come."

"In those early years," said Grandma Jo, "we didn't know any lesbians personally. As we found more women who followed the same dreams of finding another loving woman who would be an equal partner, the more strength we gained in our partnership."

Grandma Bonnie stretched her hand across to Grandma Jo's chair, touching her tenderly on the arm. Then she explained to me, "Lesbians are everywhere—in big cities, small towns and in the country, but they have been almost invisible unless they wear a pink triangle pin or a rainbow flag patch on their clothes or have a lavender bumper sticker on the cars saying, 'Meet you in Michigan in August.'"

33

"And," said Grandma Jo, "they're becoming more visible in recent years. More women's communities are developing and there are more events to attend."

"Yes, Jo," said Grandma Bonnie, turning to me again. "Lesbians could be among the teachers you know—ministers, nurses and doctors. They're factory employees and clerks, plumbers and carpenters. They are rich and poor. They serve in law enforcement, as firefighters, and in the military.

"They have many differences and talents and temperaments. They may not always be a couple living together like we live. They may be mothers or women without children, young women, middle-aged and old—sometimes they may even be married to men—and they come from every nationality, race and religion."

"But, why did the kids use that
name to tease us?" I asked Grandma
Bonnie. "I love you both, but the way
they shouted and sneered made
'lesbian' sound bad."

"Well," said Grandma Bonnie,
"that's the trouble." She motioned me
to sit closer to her and patted her hand
on the footstool.

"Some people think being a gay man or a lesbian is bad. They think that only men who love women and marry women and women who love men and marry men are how adults should live. They say that anything else is wrong. But there are a lot of people who don't fit into that pattern."

And Grandma Jo said, "Some children learn these ideas and feelings from the adults around them who speak out and often act on inaccurate and prejudiced ideas about homosexual people. "Homosexuality" is the word used to describe both gay men and lesbian women's lifestyles.

"These ideas," she continued, "have been passed along for hundreds of years by those who are afraid of others who are unlike them. These adults may have grown up learning to be uncomfortable with people of other religious or cultural beliefs or people who live lives that are different from what they've been told to live. "

Grandma Bonnie said, "Some get really angry at homosexuals, even if they don't know them. Some want to hurt them by taking away their jobs, by denying them their equal rights, by calling them names. Some of these angry people may even beat up homosexuals—or even worse. And this causes many lesbians and gay men to keep their love and their lives a secret from those they do not trust. It's called being 'in the closet,' like hiding yourself and your personal life in there. But now, more and more lesbians and gay men are coming out of the closet, showing their pride and working for their right to be themselves."

Grandma Jo was getting all pumped up and excited and said, "The benefit of being a lesbian is one of the best kept secrets ever. And it's more than just *making* love; it's *being* in love with, laughing and crying, sharing experiences together with each other and other women and children—and men we can trust.

She pounded her hand on the arm of her chair and fixed her feet firmly on the carpet. "I am proud to belong to an outstanding culture of women whose greatest goals are to love and to care for other women; to fight for what is right and fair for women and children, and most men, too; to work to stop violence, war and pollution; to create grand music and art and literature; to honor the value of Mother Earth and the Goddess in us all."

Grandma Jo's cheerleading excitement was joined by my mom clapping her hands.

"Calm down, Jo," said Grandma Bonnie. "We don't have to save the world today. We just need to comfort Amy about being teased and help her to see for herself what is worthy in people. And the more confident she is about herself, the more comfortable she will be in the future."

"Will I be a lesbian,
Grandma Bonnie?"

"That's very hard to say,
now. Probably you won't be.
There are more of what we call
'straight women' in the world
than lesbians, a lot more straight
women—like your mother and
your aunts and Jo's daughter.
Straight women and men are
called 'heterosexuals.'

"As you get older, you may have strong, caring feelings for boys who are your friends. And you may want to be close, to touch and hug them with affection. And you may also have the same feelings for girls or women and you may want to be closer to them."

Grandma Bonnie said, "Just as you make decisions about your own goals, your schooling and career, how you feel about yourself as a person, you will think about how to fulfill your emotional needs. You and your close friend need to be equally comfortable about this when you decide if it's a good time in your life to share your loving feelings with that special person."

"Whatever you decide," said Grandma Jo very carefully, "take your time and go slow. You have a lot of time to get clear in your head and to grow in understanding of your feelings in order to have worthwhile experiences of loving and sharing. And you may even change like we did. In the long run, you must be able to live the life *you* need to live."

"Let's not go too far into the future, Jo," said Grandma Bonnie, and then she spoke to me. "Remember this, Amy. Fortunately, you also have a loving family to talk with and to help you to understand and, hopefully, we'll be here for you for a long time."

"Right!" said Grandma Jo.

"We were sure lucky to have such wonderful and understanding children," said Grandma Bonnie. "Although there were some times . . . it wasn't easy. Let's say, even with our understanding families, it does take some time to get it all 'straightened' out," she said, leaning closer to me with a big smile and a raised eyebrow.

My mom said, "*Ah Huh!*"

And we all laughed together.

*****

Afterword

I want to celebrate lesbian values, courage and respectability, our uniqueness and our struggles in the pursuit of happiness.

Many lesbians' lives go uncelebrated, even unacknowledged. A profound silence casts a shadow over them and their families, friends and co-workers. Many of us have been or are so invisible, it's as if we are in a secret sorority; it seems like a miracle when we find each other. This silence denies our worth. This silence weakens our lives and our families already vulnerable to society's pressures.

Those women-loving women who reveal who they are risk themselves each day. The challenge they have accepted is sustained by the courage that it takes to be themselves.

Each woman, each situation and locale are different for each family. And families change. The two grandmothers in this story started their lives together in their forties after previous heterosexual and, by society's standards, relatively acceptable marriages for over twenty years. After finding each other, they overcame the fear of stepping beyond the heterosexual privilege to become the women they were meant to be. Their love for each other not only changed them but also the lives of everyone in both of their families. Yet after twenty years of courage and commitment to each other and to their goals, they and their family members are closely knit, healthy and happy; all their lives are, by contemporary standards, stable and successful.

This success can happen in the larger society beyond the family where all will benefit when understanding and acceptance of alternative lifestyles replace unfounded fear and intolerance. Energy is wasted by those living in secrecy and silence. It is also wasted by those divided in conflict: defenders of lesbian, gay and/or bisexual lifestyles and those demanding exclusive heterosexuality. The conflict consumes the power that could be better spent strengthening the individual, the family and society in a world without oppression and heterosexism—with people living in freedom and thriving in love.

Then we can all celebrate together.

Photo by Erin Lindquist

Together for over twenty years since they fell in love and stepped out of their "heterosexual privilege," Jeanne Arnold, right, and Barbara Lindquist founded Mother Courage Press to empower women by publishing other women's words. This is their first joint effort as author and as illustrator.

Arnold, a retired journalist and public relations workaholic, is now archiving their journals, letters and poems as a source of future stories and novels.

Lindquist, who has published three books as B. L. Holmes, continues her leadership at Mother Courage Press.

Mother Courage Press

In addition to *Amy Asks a Question*, Mother Courage publishes the following titles.

Lesbian

And Then I Met This Woman, Previously Married Women's Journeys into Lesbian Relationships by Barbee Cassingham and Sally O'Neil. A collection of 36 stories of women who were married and then fell in love with another woman. Paper $9.95

NEWS by Heather Conrad is a gripping novel of a women's computer takeover to make the empire builders and the money makers stop destroying the people and the earth. Paper $9.95

Night Lights by Bonnie Shrewsbury Arthur. More than your traditional lesbian romance, this novel tackles various issues—with a light touch that will make you laugh out loud. Paper $8.95

Singin' the Sun Up by Ocala Wings. Communicating with dolphins gives this lesbian love story a New Age twist. Paper $8.95

Mega by B. L. Holmes. Science fiction lesbian romance set against a future of giant cities and vast pollution of the Earth. Paper $8.95

Hodag Winter by Deborah Wiese. A first grade teacher is fired for being a lesbian. She and her lover and friends fight the action. Paper $8.95

Rowdy & Laughing by B. L. Holmes. She's not gay, she's rowdy and laughing. Poems encompass the joy of life and being in love. Paper $4.95

Senior Citizen by B. L. Holmes. A musical comedy, this funny and touching play explores the dual themes of rejection of the aged, gays and lesbians. Paper $8.95

Self-Help, Sexual Abuse, Prevention

Something Happened to Me by Phyllis E. Sweet, M.S. Sensitive, straightforward book designed to help children victimized by sexual or other abuse. Paper $5.95

Helping the Adult Survivor of Child Sexual Abuse, for Friends, Family and Lovers by Kathe Stark. Offers guidance for caring support people of a sexual abuse victim to help them with healing while still taking care of themselves. Paper $9.95

Why Me? Help for victims of child sexual abuse, even if they are adults now by Lynn B. Daugherty, Ph.D. Important and informative book for beginning the process of healing the psychological wounds of child sexual abuse. Paper $8.95

The Woman Inside, from Incest Victim to Survivor by Patty Derosier Barnes. This workbook is designed to help an incest victim work through pain, confusion and hurt. Paper $12.95

Warning! Dating may be hazardous to your health! by Claudette McShane. Date rape and dating abuse study emphasizes that women need not put up with any kind of abuse, are not to blame for being abused and can regain control of their lives. Paper $9.95

Fear or Freedom, a Woman's Options in Social Survival and Physical Defense by Susan E. Smith. This book realistically offers options to fear of social intimidation and fear of violent crime with an important new approach to self-defense for women. Paper $11.95

Rebirth of Power, Overcoming the Effects of Sexual Abuse through the Experiences of Others, edited by Pamela Portwood, Michele Gorcey and Peggy Sanders, is a powerful and empowering anthology of poetry and prose by survivors of sexual abuse. Paper $9.95

Travel Adventure

Women at the Helm by Jeannine Talley. Two women sell everything and begin an adventure-filled cruise around the world in a 34-foot sailboat. Paper $11.95, Hardcover $19.95

Banshee's Women, Capsized in the Coral Sea by Jeannine Talley. Continuing adventures of Talley and Smith as they are capsized and dismasted off the east coast of Australia. Paper $12.95, Hardcover $21.95

Biography

Olympia Brown, The Battle for Equality by Charlotte Coté. Biography of an unsung foremother, talented orator and the first ordained woman minister in the US who fought a life-long battle for equal rights for women. Paper $9.95, Hardcover $16.95

Humor

Womb with Views, A Contradictionary of the Enguish Language by Kate Musgrave is a delightful, more than occasionally outrageous social commentary cartoon-illustrated feminist dictionary. Paper $8.95

New Age/Healing

Welcome to the Home of Your Heart by Dorothy "Mike" Brinkman. Messages of universal love, caring and compassion given to Brinkman by an entity named Jenny. Paper $11.95

Meditations and Blessings from a Different Dimension by Dorothy "Mike" Brinkman. A healing book of channeled meditations and blessings taken from *Welcome to the Home of Your Heart*. Paper $5.95

If you don't find these books in your local book store, you may order them directly from Mother Courage Press at 1667 Douglas Ave, Racine, WI 53404. Please add $3 for postage and handling for the first book and 50¢ for each additional book.